Mickey Mouse Clubhouse

Minnie's Summer Vacation

D0038481

Based on the book written by Susan Ring
Adapted by Bill Scollon
Illustrated by Loter, Inc.

SUSTAINABLE
FORESTRY
INITIATIVE
Certified Chain of Custody
Promoting Sustainable Forestry
www.sfiprogram.org
SFI-01415
The SFI label applies to the text stock

DISNEY PRESS
New York • Los Angeles

Copyright © 2014 Disney Enterprises, Inc. All rights reserved. Published by Disney Press, an imprint of Disney Book Group. No part of this book may be reproduced or transmitted in any form or by any means, electronic or mechanical, including photocopying, recording, or by any information storage and retrieval system, without written permission from the publisher. For information address Disney Press, 1101 Flower Street, Glendale, California 91201.

First Edition 10 9 8 7 6 5 4 3 2 1
ISBN 978-1-4231-9802-4
G658-7729-4-14086

Manufactured in the USA
For more Disney Press fun, visit www.disneybooks.com

Minnie is happy.
It is summer!

What do Minnie's friends want to do?

Mickey wants to swim.

Goofy wants to fish.

Daisy wants to swing.

Pluto wants to dig.

Donald wants to hike.

Minnie wants to take pictures.

Where can they do these things?

Minnie knows.

"We will go to Star Lake!"

Goofy can fish.

Mickey can swim.

Can Daisy swing?
Minnie calls Toodles.

Toodles can help.

Now Daisy can swing!

Can Pluto dig for a bone? No!

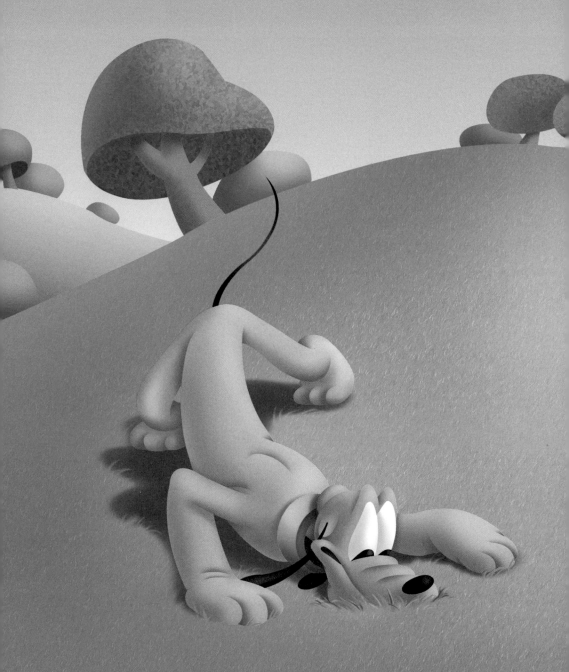

Minnie calls Toodles.

Toodles brings a map.
Now Pluto can dig!

Donald wants to hike.
Can Donald hike? Yes!

Donald can hike up a hill!

Pluto digs.
He finds a bone.

Daisy swings.

Goofy fishes.

Mickey swims.

Minnie takes pictures.
Happy summer!